Moira Duff aged three.

THE LIST

MOIRA DUFF

For Mum

1

This is how I looked.

This is how my face looked in the photo.

The Narrow Gate Church had made my face like that.

Summer, 1936

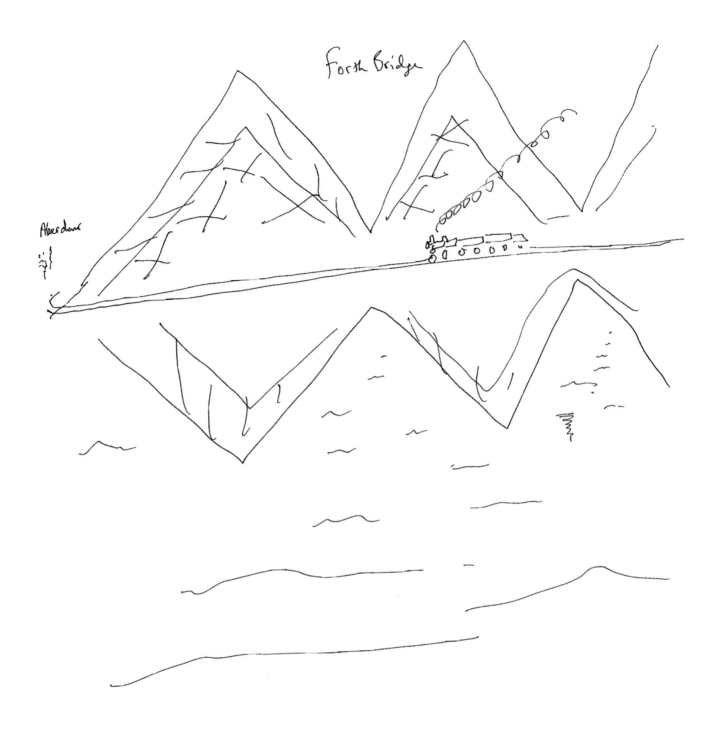

When I was one, Mummy and her bridesmaid and I, crossed the Forth

Bridge and went to Aberdour beach.

The two ladies wore calf-length silk dresses cut on the bias.

Wind blew in their hair.

They looked like film stars from Hollywood. Ginger Rogers

and Hedy Lamaar.

But as well as carrying me, Mummy also lugged bags of strange and powerful stuff.

This stuff was called Dogma.

The sun shone. The water lapped.

'Let's take a photo,' said Mummy. 'Janet! Take a photo of me and Betty!'

But my face wasn't right.

Not according to the Dogma of the Narrow Gate Church.

Mummy chucked me under the chin.

Jostled me gently.

But my face didn't change.

I think she wanted me to look like this.

But my expression stayed the same.

I knew she was angry.

My face didn't fit her Dogma.

2

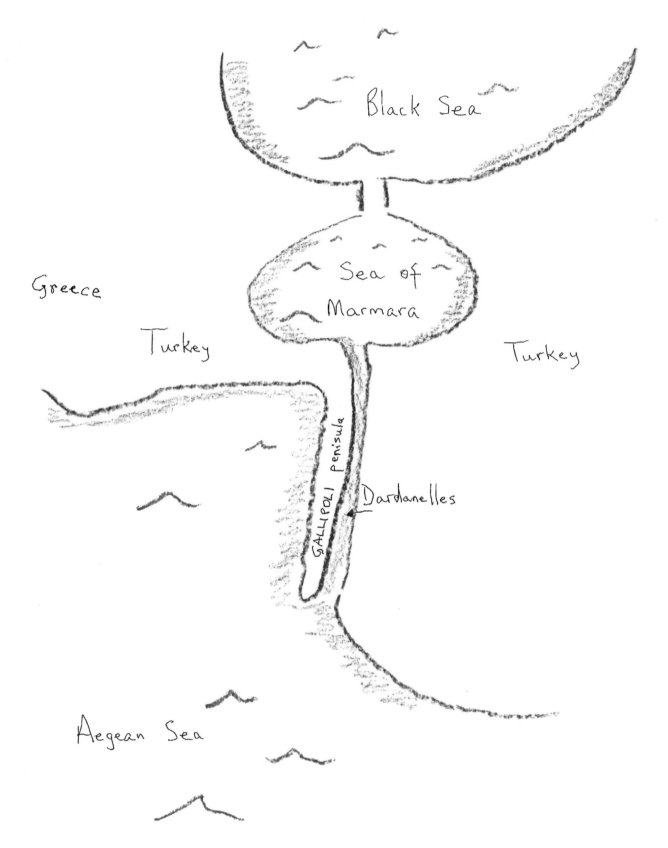

In 1915, Winston Churchill ordered thousands of men to go

to Gallipoli to fight Turkey.

My Grandad was one of them.

Grandad was in a trench.

In a trench you cook.

You move your bowels.

You shake with fear.

A rat runs over your foot.

You go over the top of the trench and fight.

But before Grandad could do that, six Turks stuck bayonets in him.

Dead Grandad left a wife.

And a child of four.

My Mum.

BRITISH RED CROSS

---AND---

ORDER OF ST. JOHN.

ENQUIRY DEPARTMENT
FOR
WOUNDED, MISSING, AND PRISONERS OF WAR

March 31st 1916.

18, Carlton House Terrace.

Sergt. Jas. L. Ross 1210, 7th Royal Scots.

Dear Madam,

Since writing to you on the 29th February, we have received the following report from L/Cpl. W. Lawrence 1369, C. Coy., 7th Royal Scots, in hospital abroad, which we think perhaps you might wish to have as it throws some light on the actual circumstances under which Sergt. Ross met his death.

L/Cpl. W. Lawrence states as follows: -

"Ross was a man of medium height, fair hair and moustache, had been through the South African War and got the Queen's Medal. His home was Leith and I think by trade he was a sawyer. On the morning of June 28 on the right of Krithia and left of Achi Baba, the battalion were retreating. The Turks were right on them in great numbers. I saw Ross in a trench with about half a dozen Turks, fighting for all he was worth. I saw him lay out two Turks and then I saw him fall, and the rest of the Turks close round him. "

If we are able to obtain any more information we will of course write to you again, and in the meantime beg to assure you once more of our deep sympathy in your loss.

Mrs. J. Ross,
45 Lorne St.,
Leith.

Yours faithfully,

Lloyd Johns

For SIR LOUIS MALLET

Grandad had no known grave.

His name, with 21,000 others, is on the thirty-metre high Memorial Obelisk

at Cape Helles on the Gallipoli Peninsula in Turkey.

It can be seen by ships passing at sea.

THEIR NAME LIVETH FOR EVERMORE

Two months after the bayonets killed her son, the mother of the dead soldier

left her home in Sutherland and moved to Edinburgh.

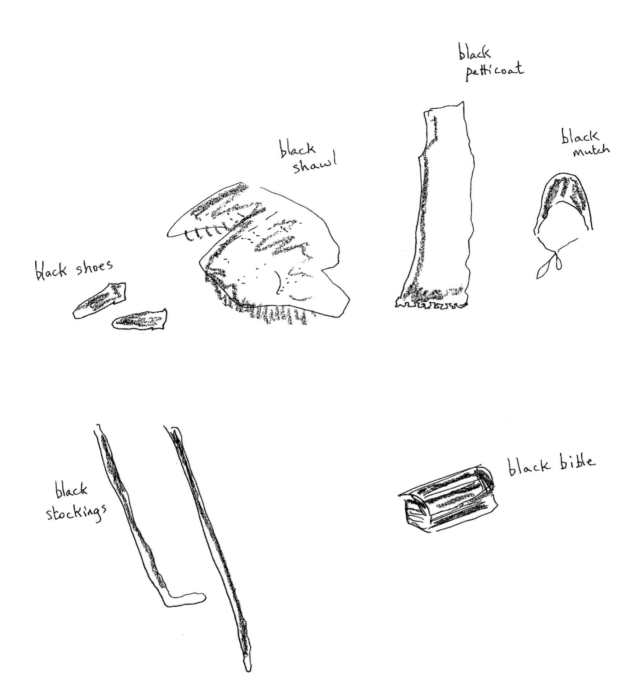

black petticoat

black shawl

black mutch

black shoes

black stockings

black bible

Moved, with her black shoes, black bible, petticoats, black mutch, knitted stockings, black dress and shawl - moved in with the dead man's wife and child.

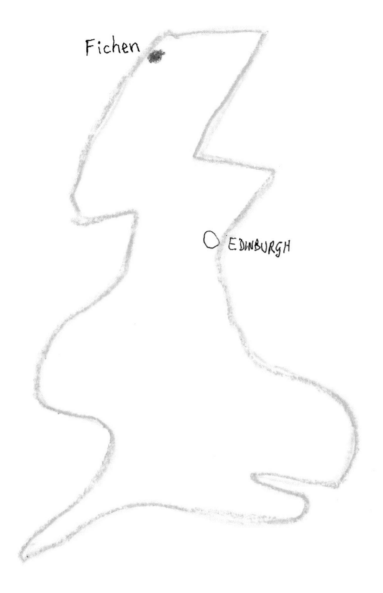

Fichen

○ EDINBURGH

On the way the old woman thought of all she'd leave behind.

Farewell to her village, Fichen.

The rented house.

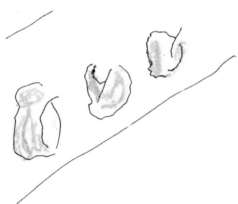

Her cow and cabbage patch.

Leave the mountains. Stac Polly. Assynt.

Worst she'd lose her Church.

The elect and blessed Church.

Or as it was known to privileged Elders, God's blessed Church of Ceart and

Cearr.

Ceart and Cearr are the Gaelic for Right and Wrong.

Ceart (pronounced Karsht).

Cearr (pronounced Kar).

The Founder died in 1586.

Date of birth not known.

Nor his name.

Records were lost in a fire.

In Memory of
blessed John Knox's
visit 1530

But a stained glass window bears the name John Knox.

In the Narrow Gate Church the hair on the heads of the women never

touched their coat collars.

3

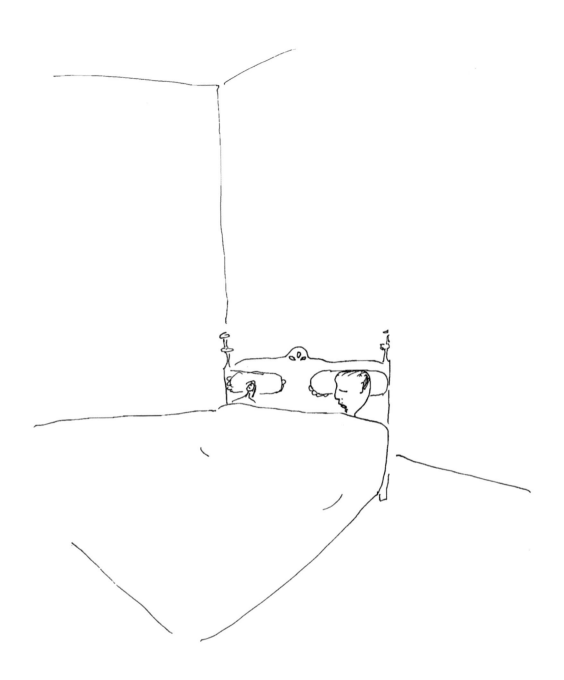

For eleven years, the old woman slept with the girl in the kitchen recess.

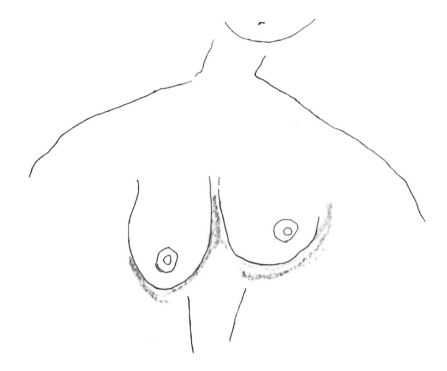

For eleven years, the old woman taught Mummy the rules of the Narrow

Gate believers.

Things like "Thou shalt have no fun."

"Always stir soup in a clockwise direction."

"Breasts are disgusting."

"Thou shalt not look in a mirror."

But also imbued in Mummy, a total hatred of Turks.

Drove it deep.

The lessons continued.

Till Mummy was sixteen, then Sutherland Granny died.

The National Museum of Scotland took the religious lady's mutch.

The black mutch had never been off the poor woman's head.

The girl grew up.

She met John at the tennis club.

When she was twenty-three, they got married.

Margaret and John were married in a cathedral.

It was correct, right, and good to be married in a cathedral.

Mummy squashed down the cathedral's "wrongness".

After the honeymoon, as well as a new cooker and a new clock, Margaret

took her Narrow Gate baggage into the marriage.

Two years later, on a Sunday evening, a baby was born to Margaret and John.

This baby was me.

So, the child born on the Sabbath Day, is bonny and blithe and good and gay.

The omens were excellent.

4

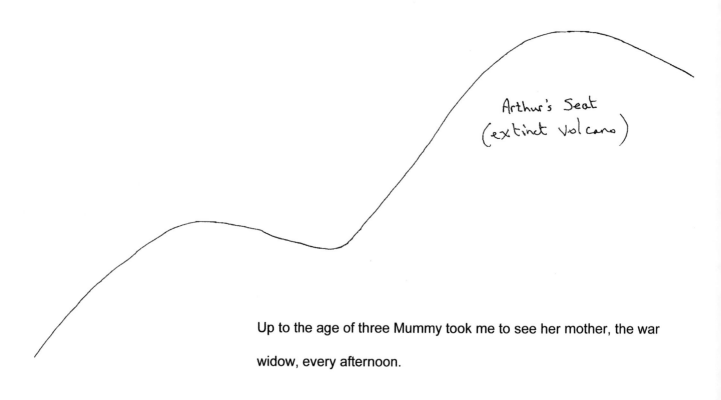

Arthur's Seat
(extinct volcano)

Up to the age of three Mummy took me to see her mother, the war

widow, every afternoon.

They'd always been close.

The house sat on the slopes of Arthur's Seat.

Grandma's house

Cosy Grandma Ross could go weak with laughter.

She had an amputated leg and a sliding cupboard where she kept chocolates.

Grandma Ross

Aunty Kate

Aunty Nell

Aunty Kate and Aunty Nell lived with Grandma.

Unmarried.

Very overweight ladies.

But fine upright postures.

One day in their garden I screamed and screamed at the

Michaelmas daisies.

They were taller than I was.

At Grandma Ross's house I also heard that bathrooms were disgusting.

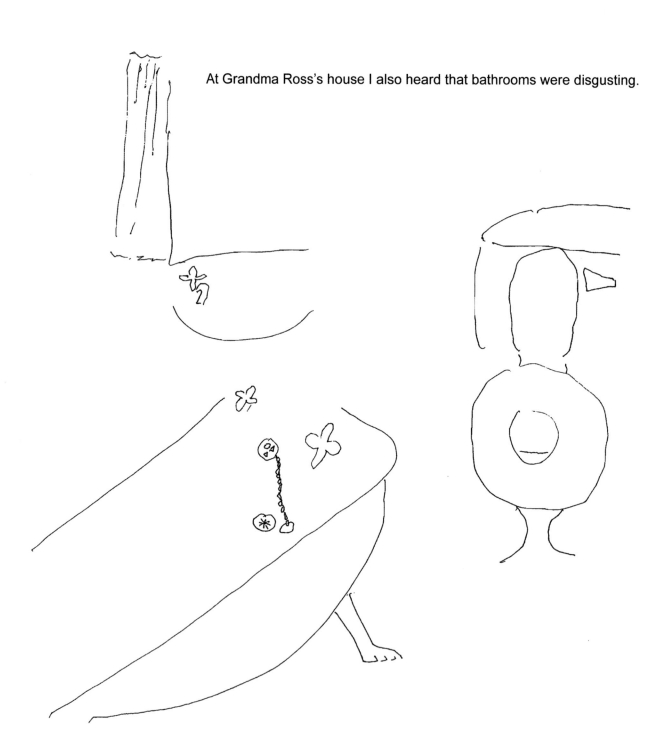

Mummy gave me a frown.

5

When I was three we moved to Leeds.

Soon after the move I learnt another bad thing.

I used to sit on my Daddy's knee.

But no-one knew that this put Mummy through torture due to her

childhood conditionings and teachings.

Really Mummy will have wanted to scream!

But the message got across.

Daddy got the message.

I never sat on Daddy's knee again.

The War Years

6

When I was four World War 2 started.

Daddy's flapping trousers went round the corner of the Vergen's garden, off to war.

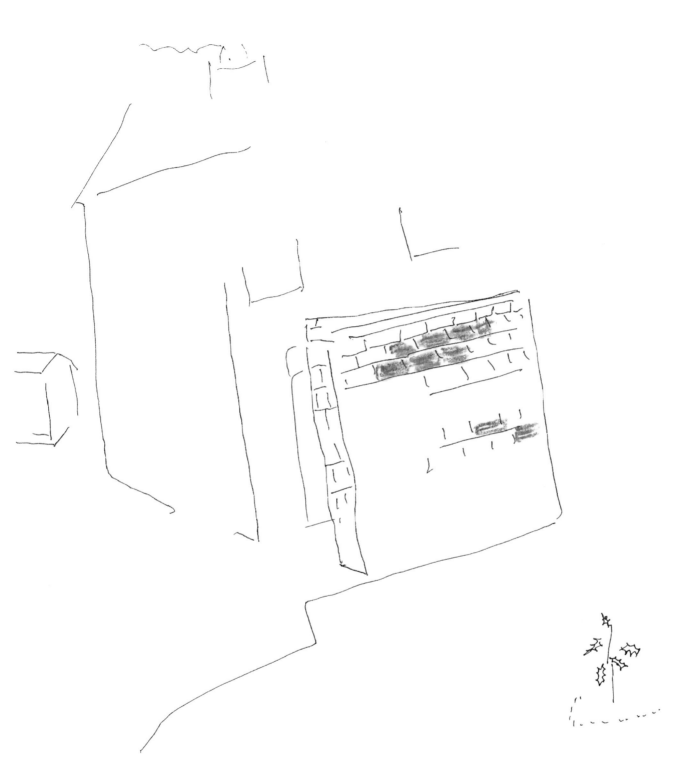

But before he went, Daddy had a brick wall built at the front door.

To protect us from bomb blast.

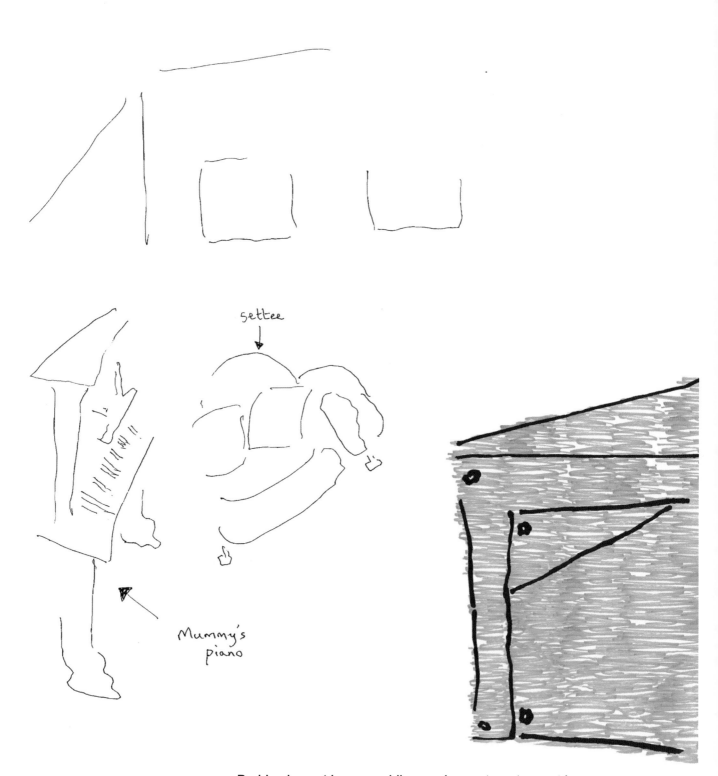

settee

Mummy's
piano

Daddy also got heavy welding engineers to put a cast iron

shelter in the sitting room.

Mummy's Pleyel piano had to get moved out of the way.

And the uncut moquette settee.

My little brother and sister stood still watching the violent green installation.

Mummy seemed to be cut to pieces with a hacksaw.

No-one else had brick walls on their doorstep.

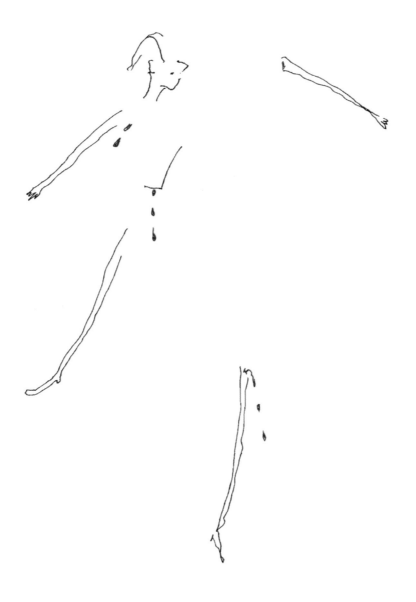

I held a big pink pottery rabbit Daddy had given me.

'Look after the others,' he said.

My brother and sister weren't given anything.

Mummy called me highly strung.

I absorbed that.

I accepted the label "Highly Strung".

Like a price tag.

I slept with Mummy after Daddy went.

Like a teddy.

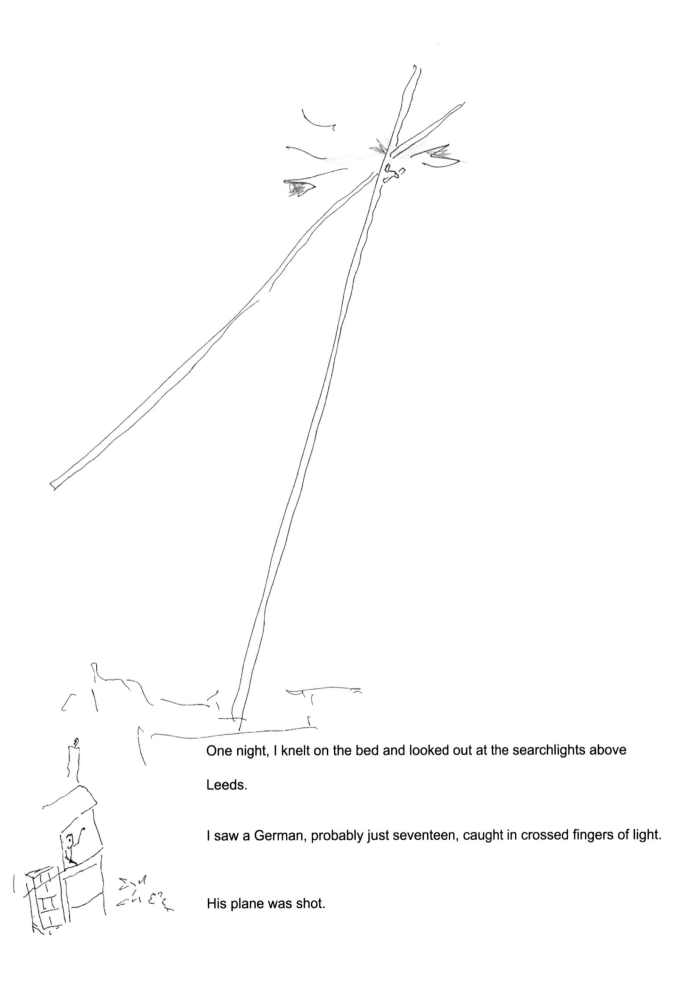

One night, I knelt on the bed and looked out at the searchlights above

Leeds.

I saw a German, probably just seventeen, caught in crossed fingers of light.

His plane was shot.

His fingers and toes and nose fell onto the allotments.

I told Mummy.

I got another label.

"Too much imagination!"

Next day I rushed into the house when a German bomber passed over our

garden and looked down on me on my swing.

The pilot looked into my eyes.

propellor

Another night with all the sirens and bombs I couldn't sleep.

Then I thought I would.

'Mummy!' I called from the landing, 'I'm just going off to sleep.'

'That's fine, Betty. Goodnight.'

But I didn't sleep.

Then I thought I would.

'I didn't go to sleep last time, Mummy,' I called again from the landing. 'I'm

definitely going to sleep now.'

'Fine! Right! Goodnight!'

But sleep evaded me.

Then I felt it coming again.

Nervously I padded out to the landing banister.

'Sorry, but I didn't go to sleep that time either, Mummy. But I am now - '

'BETTY! Will you GET into bed and STAY there!

I don't want to hear from you again!'

Mummy played the piano during the war. Squeezed past the green air-raid

shelter.

I lay in the rosewood double bed.

Zdenko Fibich floated up from the sitting room.

The pain of Zdenko Fibich's *Poem.*

It just about killed me.

Mummy taught me to play.

We got on like a house on fire.

Two peas in a pod.

When I was six I was put to a piano teacher.

There were thick curtains.

I cried at every visit.

The piano teacher hit me and hit me.

She would scream, 'You're just crying because you're scared your Daddy's going to be killed in the War aren't you! Say it! Say it!'

She bent my fingers back.

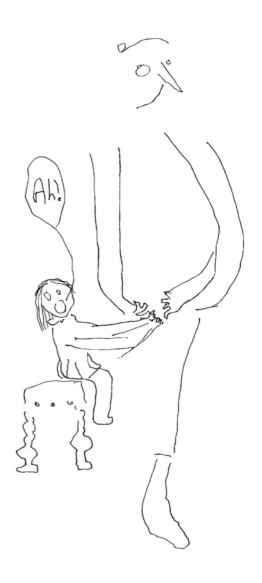

Miss Sumpter was her name.

After the lesson I stood, with my music case, in the alcove at the front

between us and the Vergens. Till the wind blew the redness off my face.

Mummy was up to her elbows in Rinso at the back.

I didn't tell her.

I knew she'd think I'd done something to annoy Miss Sumpter.

'Get changed. Out to play.'

7

That summer we went to Grandma Ross's house.

Aunty Nell showed me her greenhouse.

Aunty Nell watered her tomatoes from a watering can.

The water was brown.

'What do you put in your watering can, Aunty Nell?'

'What's in there comes from sheep on the hill,' said Aunty Nell.

I couldn't ask Mummy how Aunty Nell grabbed hold of the sheep and stuck her watering can under them.

It wasn't till many years later I discovered Aunty Nell collected sheep's poo.

Put it in her watering can. Added water.

It became fertiliser.

That same holiday we went to Portobello with Mummy's cousin's wife.

Annie and family. Eight of us on the tram.

Aunty Annie's husband Willie had been done for fraud.

But now they were separated.

Aunty Annie was acceptable again.

My brother had knitted trunks.

The crotch was nearly down at his feet.

'Tuck the top into the elastic,' Mummy shouted.

My little sister's stomach stuck out.

'Stop frowning,' called Mummy.

One of Aunty Annie's children had a club foot.

I didn't know what a club foot meant.

I knew what a club was.

You swung a club and hit people with it.

We weren't allowed to stare.

Her sister had curly hair.

truncheon to club people

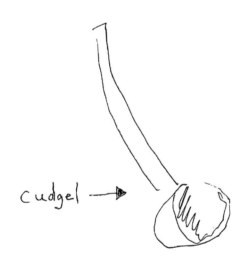

cudgel →

I don't know if they took the club foot off.

I don't remember noticing her in the water.

I don't know anything about it.

It filled my mind.

I just couldn't stop thinking about those words.

But I couldn't ask anybody.

Everyone had a good time.

Throwing themselves in the waves.

Getting a shell off the sea bed.

Screaming with fun.

I could only bear to go in up to my ankles.

The girl with the club foot and my brother with his sagging trunks and my

sister with her tummy, all ran back for towels and jam sandwiches.

I had come out almost dry.

We went up King's Road for the tram.

I'd made our family a laughing stock.

This was forbidden.

That evening I asked Grandma if I could look through her chest of drawers.

Grandma never minded. I found it greatly comforting to be allowed into

someone's private life. Old corsets and pants and papers, football pools,

keys, stockings. My brother and sister never did.

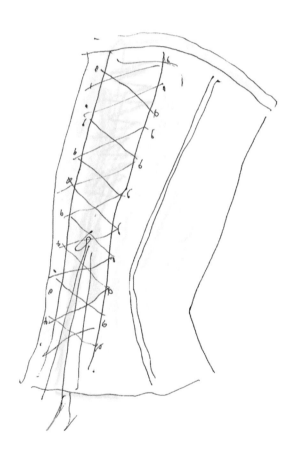

When I went downstairs I said to Mummy who folded towels,

'What did the number "7th", mean in that newspaper cutting?'

Mummy's eyes went in several directions at once.

'Battalion', I heard.

But she'd left the room.

Near the end of that holiday my little brother and sister caught chicken-pox.

We couldn't go on the train.

They were in quarantine.

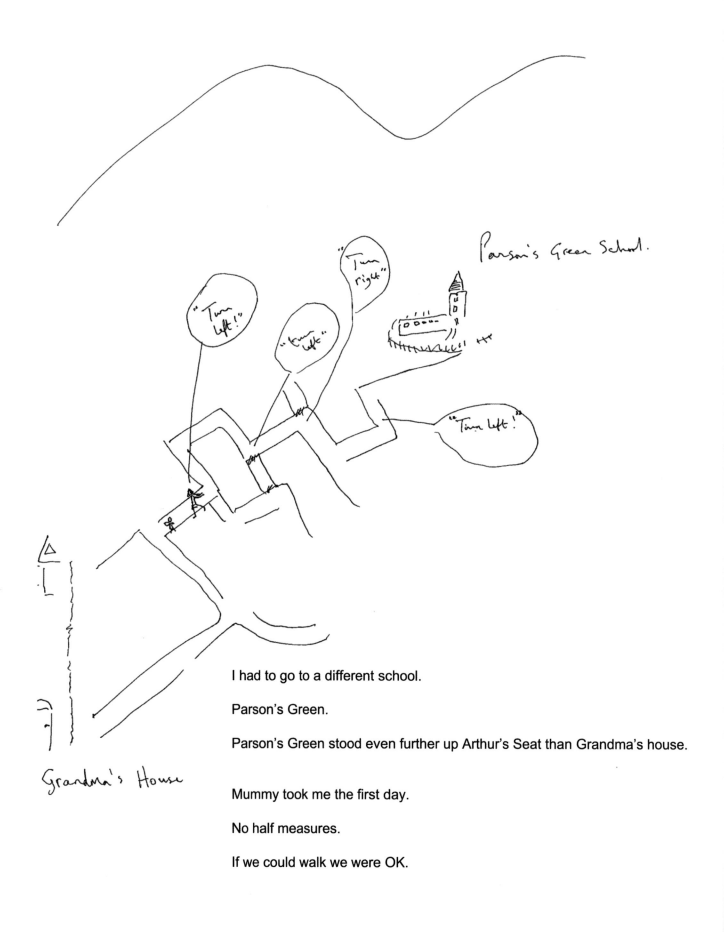

I had to go to a different school.

Parson's Green.

Parson's Green stood even further up Arthur's Seat than Grandma's house.

Mummy took me the first day.

No half measures.

If we could walk we were OK.

Next day I went by myself.

I couldn't remember.

I turned right when I should have turned left.

Then I should have turned right.

It was Snakes and Ladders.

I was late.

The janitor heard me.

I was nearly in tears.

In the cloakroom the string of my purse had got tangled with my gas mask.

I put the strap of my schoolbag back the original way to get at the cord of

my purse.

The whole jumble of the harnesses, strings and straps were wound round

me. Buckles dug through material. Loose thread was coming off a coat

button.

The janitor got everything undone.

I was breathless with wanting to cry.

Before the summer finished and now that the chicken-pox was over

Mummy took photos for Daddy in the war.

When it was my turn she had an important thing to ask.

It stole my birthright clean away.

Some months later during the school holidays, when

Mummy was occupied sticking pins of the German

line in the map on the wall, I told her I had something to say.

She didn't turn round.

'I just wanted to tell you I love you fifth best in the world,' I said.

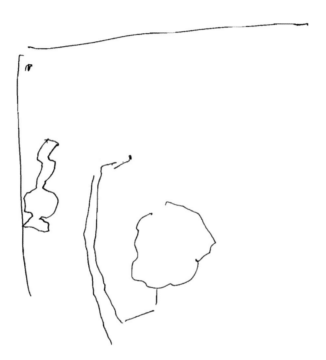

She didn't say anything.

I said, 'I love God best,

Jesus second,

the Holy Spirit third,

Grandma Ross fourth,

and you and Daddy fifth.'

I actually would have put Mummy sixth.

But I didn't want to hurt her.

She made no response at all.

8

One of the first things was, Daddy got the brick wall on the front doorstep removed.

Daddy gave me a pink pottery baby rabbit

to go with the big one.

I couldn't look at him.

'You did a good job,' he said.

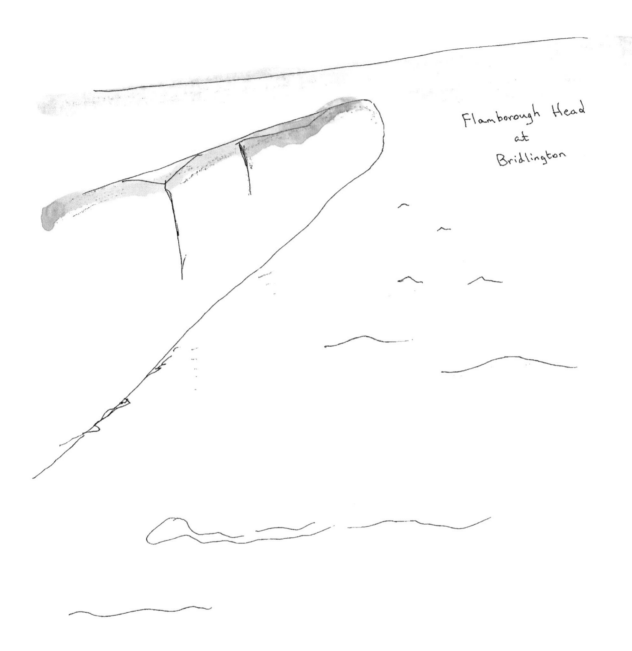

Flamborough Head
at
Bridlington

After the mess of the wall was over Daddy took us to Bridlington.

Hurray!!

Marvellous!

WONDERFUL!!

Daddy said there was a toilet on the boarding house landing.

Before we went to the beach we all had to use it.

After which Daddy would give us a penny.

I went last.

My brother and sister must have managed.

But I couldn't 'go'.

Daddy knocked and whispered.

There was a queue of people from Hunslet on the stair.

I felt terrible.

It hadn't been such a good idea of Daddy's.

Mummy's face was

frozen with embarrassment.

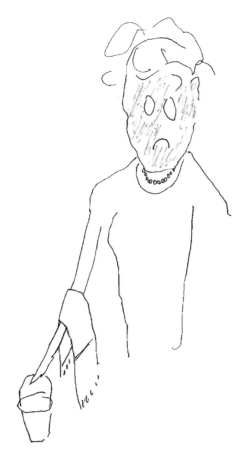

I heard Daddy gently tell Mummy that he wasn't going to battle beside

Montgomery and Eisenhower, help at the liberation of Belsen, get his socks off

and sink into a deckchair at Bridlington, for someone to then need the toilet.

Sunday we went to church.

Mummy blushed at the loudness of Daddy's singing. I felt the same.

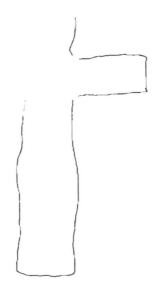

The minister gave an excellent sermon.

His words moved me more than I had ever felt before.

Mummy gave me a look.

Before bed Daddy made us say the Lord's Prayer. Then add a little bit.

Like, "God bless sick animals."

That night my sister said, "tem-pew-tation."

I snorted and had to grapple for my hanky.

My brother was next.

Then it was my turn.

I had done it again.

I'm sure Mummy had wanted to scream, 'WHAT cross!'

After Bridlington, Daddy bought a dog.

A bargain at Leeds Market by the bus station.

Full pedigree wire-haired fox terrier.

Vertical tail.

A real find, Daddy told himself on the tram.

It fell to me to take it walks.

Mummy was always busy.

We called it Kim.

Daddy was on business in Cleethorpes.

It fought other dogs.

Went for their throats.

I didn't tell Mummy.

The house was stinking.

Mummy had to boil lights* for Kim's meals.

Wipe up muddy footprints.

* lungs

The attacks on other dogs were terrible.

I'd been told to make Kim walk 'at heel'.

I tapped him on the nose.

But he just charged into the next fight.

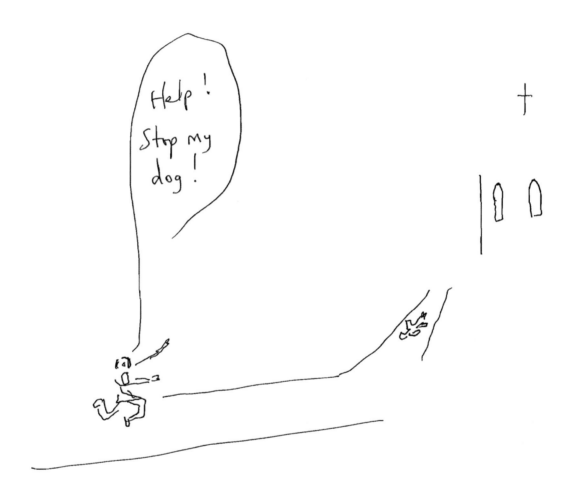

We had Kim about a month.

And then he had a fit and ran off.

I went screaming after him.

By the Church of England school and the tram track.

The vet diagnosed distemper and hysteria.

Kim was put down.

Mummy opened all the windows.

9

But my piano playing still continued.

Kim had used to lie next to a back leg of the stool.

Lessons stopped with Miss Sumpter.

I got a scholarship to another school.

A bust of Artur Schnabel stood on the piano.

I sat in the new room with my toes curled up.

Mummy called my feet "big".

I crammed my feet into too-small shoes.

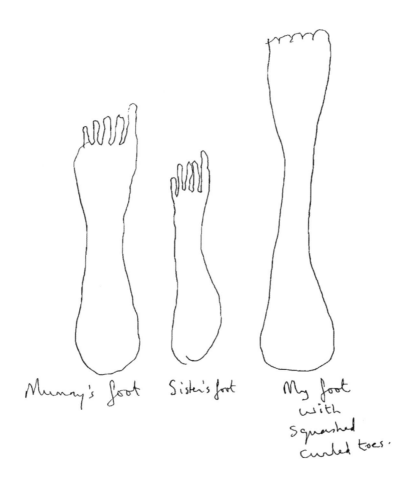

Mummy's foot   Sister's foot   My foot
with
squashed
curled toes.

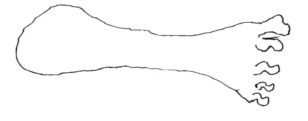

side view
of mine

I needed a "big" velour hat for my new school.

Mummy explained in the shop that I had a big head.

The uniform was green.

Green didn't suit me.

It was about this time that Vevina Cowie moved into our street.

I'd just had my first bike puncture.

Vevina's Daddy knew mine.

Mummy couldn't mention Vevina's name.

Or even look at her.

It was so weird.

I didn't mention Vevina's name either.

Daddy behaved as if her name was Jennifer or Susan.

The next idea Daddy had was a procedure to be carried out before bedtime.

'From now on,' said Dad, 'I would like you kiddies to give your mother and me a kiss before you go to bed. All right?'
He gave a generous smile.

Mummy's knitting speeded up.

'We'll start tonight.'

It only lasted one night.

Perhaps Mummy said it seemed un-natural.

It definitely felt peculiar.

One morning my mother said we were going to buy a hockey stick.

But the sports shop was opposite the dentist.

I couldn't concentrate in the sports shop.

At the last check-up, we'd been told, if something wasn't done, I'd have too many teeth for my jaw.

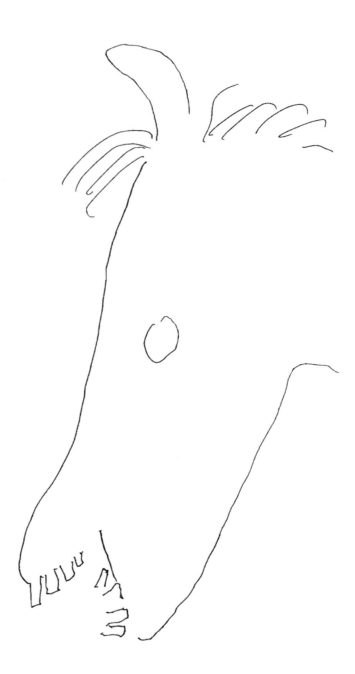

In the waiting room Mummy turned over pictures of horses in a *Picture Post*

to calm me.

I shook violently. People stared.

In the night I woke when a big red slug came out of my mouth.

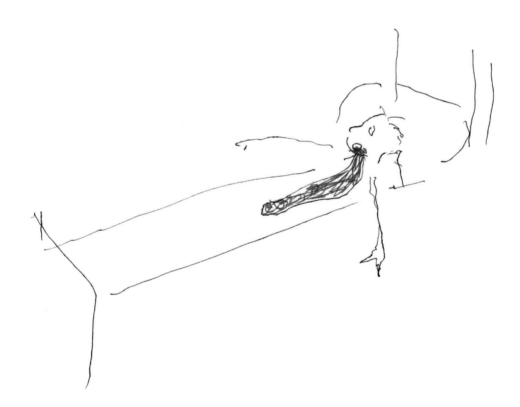

I screamed for Mummy.

But Mummy told me not to be silly.

It was just a clot.

She changed the sheet.

A further thing that had to be seen to was my hair.

The shop was in Boar Lane.

The shop's name was Pantene's. Like pants.

My brother and sister giggled all the way on the tram.

Mummy put on a brave face.

I tried to too.

I didn't know why she'd picked the place.

'Please thin my daughter's hair.'

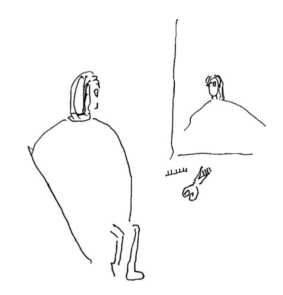

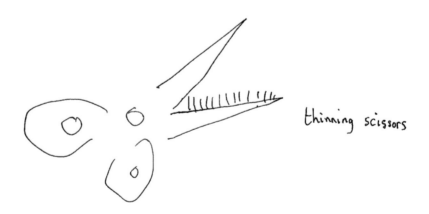

thinning scissors

In a further effort to make me look decent, I got a perm.

My unpermed hair Mummy had called "lank".

It was pointed out that it was a "cold" perm.

Not a frizz.

I squirmed at the expense.

Then a boy fell in love with me.

He was tall and good-looking.

He asked me to the cinema.

I said I'd ask my mother.

I thought she'd faint.

But she recovered.

'Certainly go! Oh certainly go!'

He was the son of respectable neighbours.

'That's very very nice! Oh DO go!'

Back row of the cinema

It seemed Jeff wanted to do things other than watch the film.

10

Just before the summer holidays Mummy announced we were moving

back to Scotland.

I was told to find a good home for my chinchilla rabbit, Flopsy.

'No room in the removal van,' said Mummy.

I tried to remember if Mummy had ever met Flopsy.

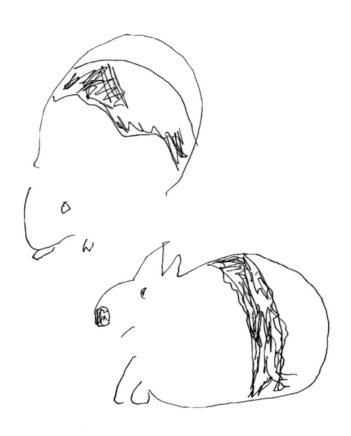

I was told to find a new owner for my guinea pigs.

I had to leave the Guides.

Jeff asked me to go for a walk in Roundhay Park.

I wore a diagonal stripe dress Mummy had kindly made.

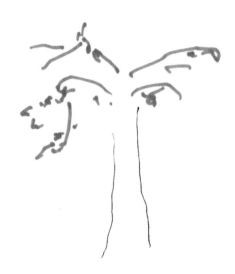

In the park Jeff suggested we sit down.

But then he lay on top of me. And put his hand over the chest area of my

diagonal striped dress.

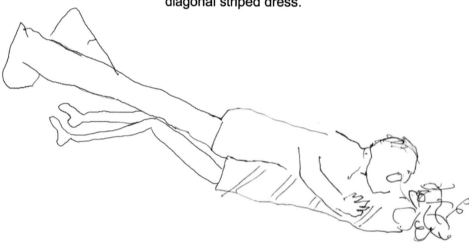

I didn't know what he thought he was doing!

But I knew he'd now completely gone off me.

Perhaps I shouldn't have stopped him doing what he was doing.

11

In Aberdeen everyone had net curtains.

Kept closed.

The school was like the armed forces.

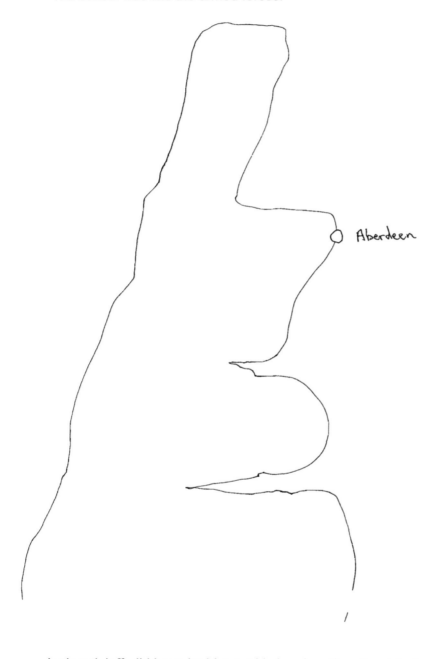

Aberdeen

I missed Jeff. I'd have let him put his hand on the other bit of my chest if he
could have walked up the road, here in Scotland.

At school in Scotland the girls all laughed at me.

I said, 'boota'.

They all said, 'butta'.

Screamingly funny.

They made me Buttons in their pantomime.

Mummy blew up.

I was sent to elocution lessons.

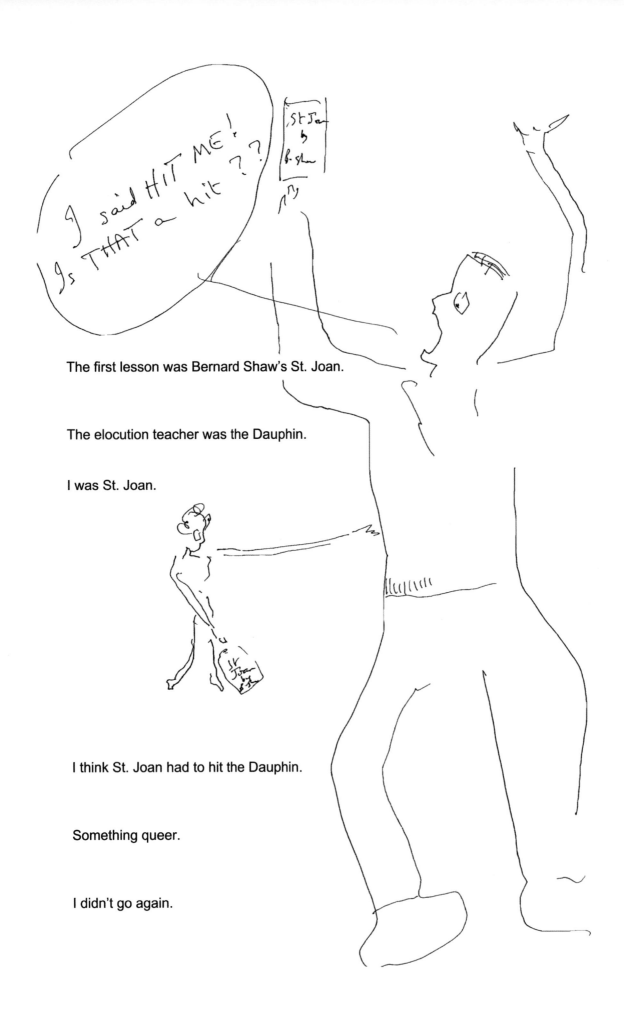

The first lesson was Bernard Shaw's St. Joan.

The elocution teacher was the Dauphin.

I was St. Joan.

I think St. Joan had to hit the Dauphin.

Something queer.

I didn't go again.

I was still fourteen.

It was time for me to be confirmed.

A lady with a daughter with a large bust
lent my mother a white silk dress.

I had no bust.

The dress hung like an empty parachute.

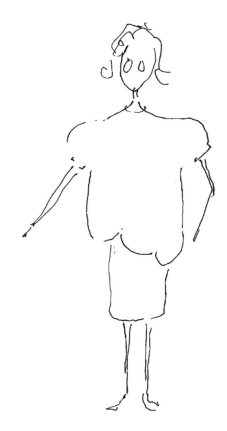

When the Bishop put his hands on my head, a dove flew down above me

then flew away again.

I didn't know why that happened.

Mummy never said anything.

But she certainly did a few days later.

In the middle of the night I thought the house was on fire.

But it wasn't a fire.

Just smoke from kindling drying.

I could have sworn I had seen flames.

Mummy was blazing.

'If there IS another time, but let's hope that'll never be,' she said, 'maybe

you could quietly knock on our bedroom door and speak calmly and quietly?

Listening are you?'

I left it a week or two after the fire fiasco.

Before I broached another subject.

'Could I have a bra please, Mum?'

I tried out the words in my bedroom.

Each word felt like molten lead in my throat.

I tried, 'Please could I have a bra, Mum?'

Then I tried, 'Mum, I think I need a bra.'

Then I mouthed, 'Scuse me Mum, all the girls in my class have a bra.'

I got it out.

She was making junket.*

'I'll see to it,' she said.

*A dish of sweetened and flavoured curds of milk.

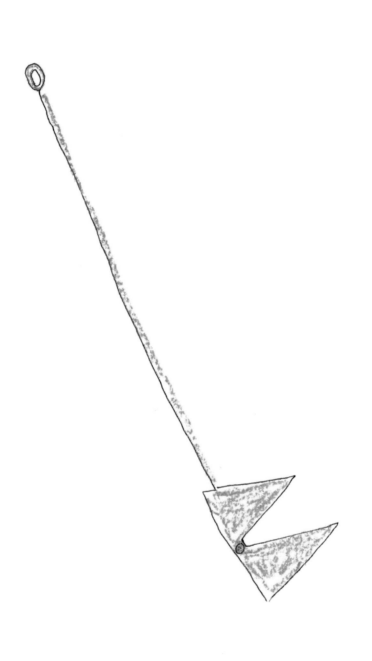

It lay on my bed.

Peach silk.

The long strap came round your back and fastened on the button at the

front.

The cups were pointed pyramids.

I didn't know where the shoulder straps were. I was too stressed.

I told Mummy it was a bit big.

'I'll alter it,' she said.

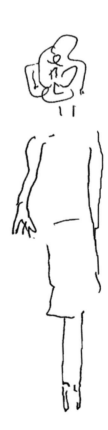

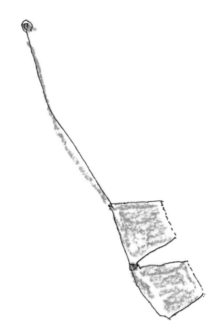

She'd run her sewing machine right through the points. And snipped them off.

Now they looked like octagons.

'Daddy sent it from Belgium,' she said.

And wiped down the sink.

12

At the beginning of the school holidays I went to Edinburgh. On my way to Filey.

I told Aunts Kate and Nell I would buy a bra in Darling's.

But the words were hardly out of my mouth before Aunty Nell missed a

chair, and lay on the floor, and in between screams of laughter she asked

what I thought I'd put in it.

So I was a Punch and Judy show.

Ha ha ha.

Was I her great-niece?

Or just a fool with teensie weenzie breasts.

Ha ha ha ha ha.

I did buy one.

The smallest you could get.

It nearly stopped my blood circulation.

The bra was grey after three weeks in a caravan at Filey.

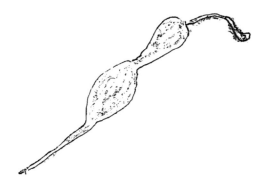

I don't know how they'll have discussed such a thing but Daddy had to give

me my sex education.

Mummy was "unable to".

I only heard "penis" and "erect" and "vagina".

And felt ill.

I heard a sperm could even jump off your thigh, wriggle in, and make a

baby.

Sperm
entering me

On the same subject I should perhaps say my periods hadn't started.

When I was fourteen they didn't come.

Nobody said anything.

When I was fifteen they didn't come.

Nobody said anything.

When I was sixteen they didn't come.

Nobody said anything.

Suddenly, at nearly eighteen, there was a blob of red in the toilet.

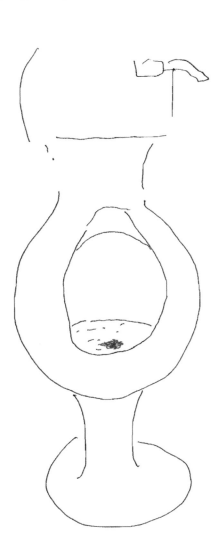

Mummy put down the potato peeler.

There was no opening a bottle of champagne.

No hug.

'Wait there.'

She brought a pile of dusters.

I felt
like this.

'Stick these in your pants. Go back to school. I'll get other things later.'

We never met eyes.

Or this.

Nothing much happened in the next three years.

But I became friends with Sonia.

All the girls loved Sonia.

All the boys did too.

I didn't see why the boys did.

Sonia and I were very close.

We giggled under our desk lids.

We took a black cashmere jumper and torn black stockings out of

Sonia's stepmother's waste basket.

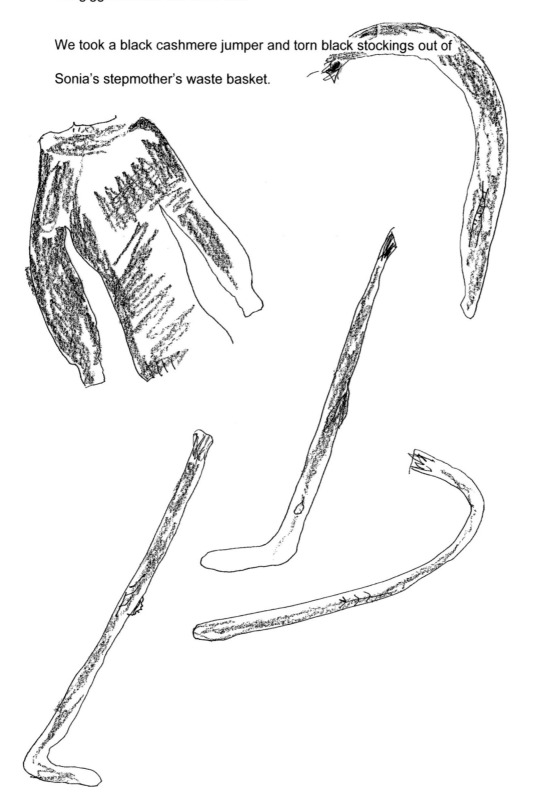

In my nylon stockings I met a Swiss boy. Roger Klatter.

I passed my driving test and drove Roger around in Daddy's car.

Mummy had said she would never go in a car with me driving.

Sonia and I trained to be teachers.

I wasn't very good at it.

In a class of thirty, twenty-seven of them would be at the toilet.

The Headmaster came in.

When I was nearly twenty one I decided to lose my you-know-what.

Sonia did too.

She and I set off with a T-shirt and toothpaste each for the south of France.

To drive a coach and six through the rules of home.

It was like pulling super-glue off a wall.

← Monte Carlo

good looking
Surgeon

Ugly friend

On the road to Monte Carlo we met two men from Oxford.

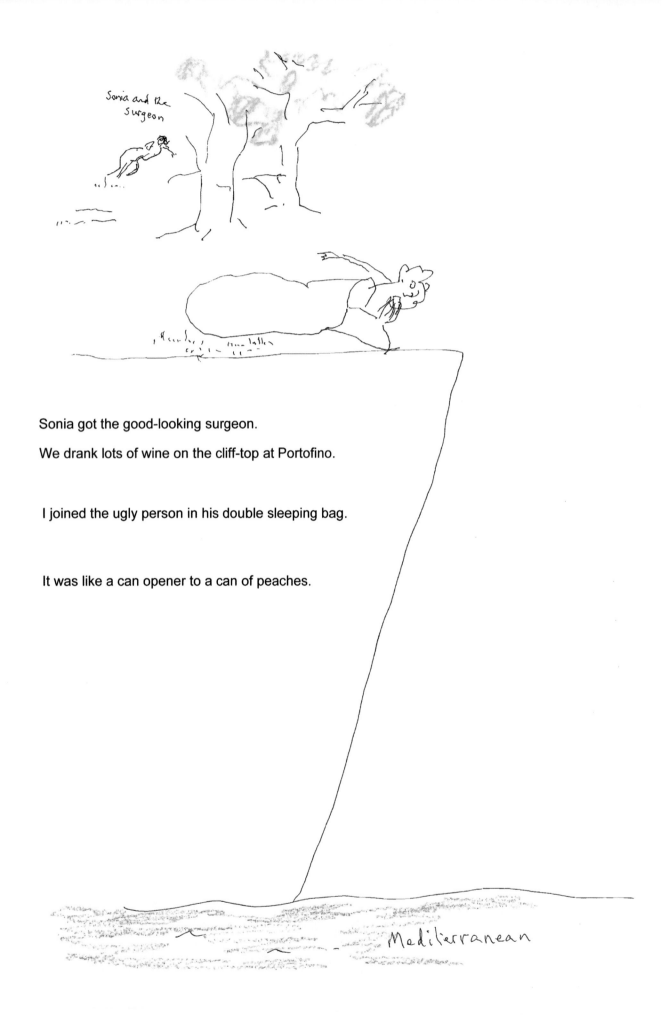

Sonia got the good-looking surgeon.

We drank lots of wine on the cliff-top at Portofino.

I joined the ugly person in his double sleeping bag.

It was like a can opener to a can of peaches.

The men invited us to travel on to Rome with them.

I said we were going back to the UK. We'd done what we came for.

Sonia then said I might like to know she'd done it lots of times.

I was shocked to the core.

I felt betrayed and devastated.

The insides of my thighs were inflamed.

I don't think Sonia's were.

My other thought was if I'd got pregnant.

If I was, Mummy would be relieved that at least the man was British

and had brains and straight legs.

13

Six weeks after I got back I rushed into marriage.

I said I'd go to the North Pole with him.

I didn't say I wore jumpers in the summer. Edward was glamorous. He

smoked Senior Service. Been a radio officer in the Indian Ocean. Owned a

car and wore a suit. There was a sixteen year difference in our ages.

We lived in Elgin. The marriage was disastrous.

Two boys were born.

Andrew and Stephen.

Then a third son, Martin, who died aged a month.

I was torn to shreds.

Martin was cremated in the family christening dress.

I sent his ashes to Mummy.

Mummy had a fit.

Aunty Nell had made the christening dress.

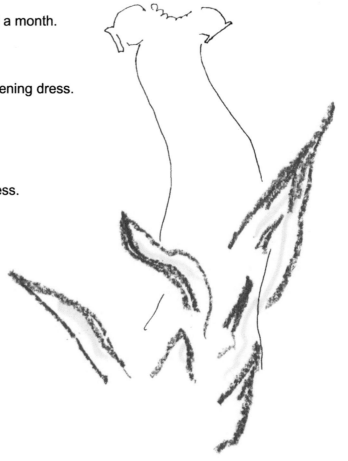

For some reason Edward regularly called me a dirty, filthy, slimy person.

Every day he called me it.

I thought of snails.

Andrew and Stephen were taught to shout it. And laugh.

They shouted it at the postman.

Edward egged them on.

But things became an avalanche.

Edward put Stephen in a bath of scalding water.

The avalanche was roaring. He broke Andrew's arm on the washing

machine paddle.

Andrew's mouth wide open.

He locked them in a shed for a freezing day with only bread and water.

I sat with round shoulders at a lawyer's.

'Life is mad,' I said.

I got a divorce.

Edward let me have the house.

He was going to Arizona.

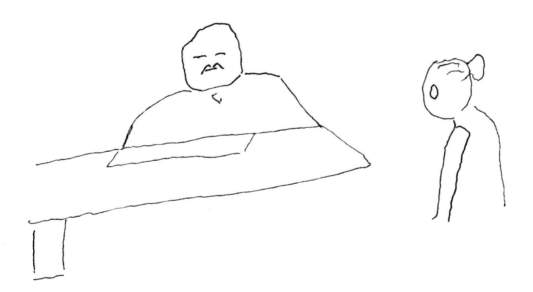

We moved back to Aberdeen. I married again.

My mother thought Georgie was a wonderful man.

My new husband had whaling ancestry.

He was going to need it.

Boys by my first marriage

From day one, Andrew and Stephen held Georgie in contempt. He was the

incomer. Mummy was theirs, not his. They called Georgie an idiot.

Jealousy filled them to the brim.

Then when Keith was born, and three years later Eric, I was shared out even more.

Around then, Mummy asked if I could 'do something' about my baby Martin's

ashes.

The urn had been behind the altar at the family church.

I asked Mummy if she wanted to come with me and scatter them on the

sea.

But she didn't.

I scattered my baby's ashes myself.

But we still had the piano in common.

Mummy had the grand Daddy had bought, and her Pleyel.

I had two pianos in my house.

Georgie gave me anything I wanted.

It was the only area where Mummy and I....

 where Mummy and I........

 touched each other's soul.

My brother and sister touched Mummy's soul all the time.

Keith and Eric were relentlessly teased by the older two.

Keith soaked it up like a sponge.

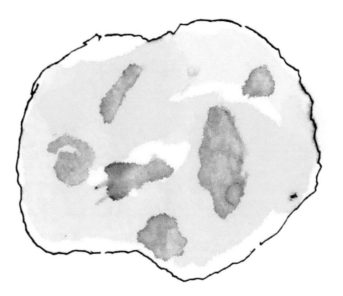

Eric was a bouncing ball.

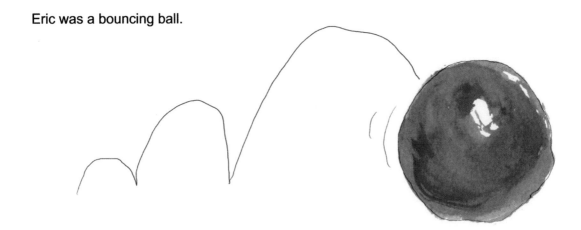

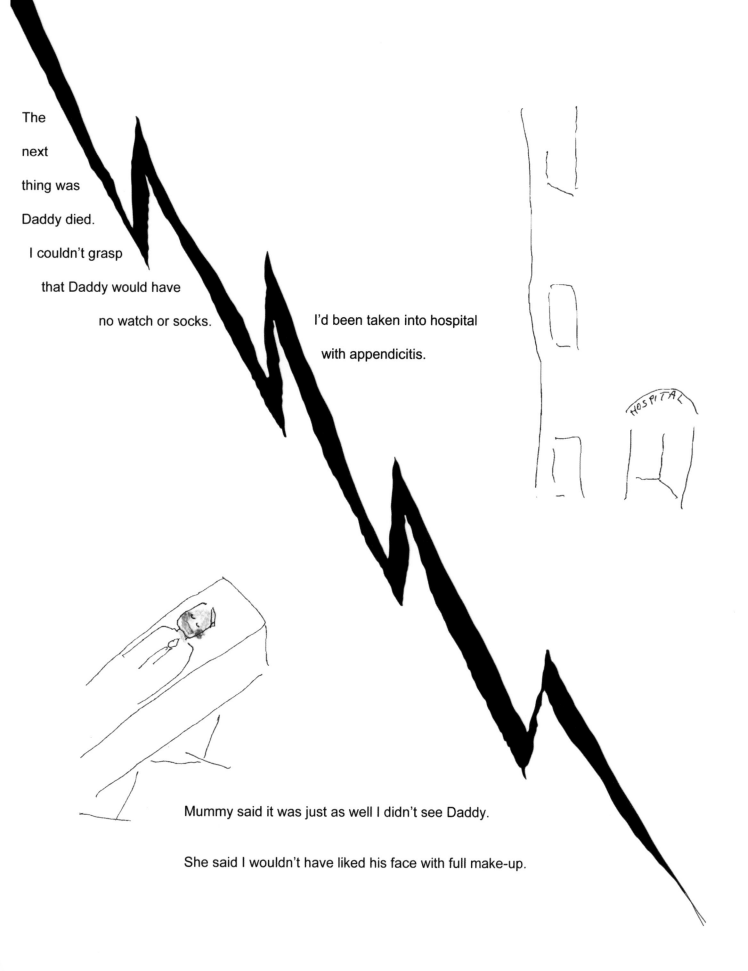

The

next

thing was

Daddy died.

I couldn't grasp

that Daddy would have

no watch or socks.

I'd been taken into hospital

with appendicitis.

Mummy said it was just as well I didn't see Daddy.

She said I wouldn't have liked his face with full make-up.

14

I struggled with my life.

The older boys were crushed by their Grandad's death.

He had been more of a father to them than

Edward had been.

Georgie kept me going.

He read, "O my Luve's like a red, red rose."

He read, "Ae Fond Kiss."

My older boys however, were becoming back-breaking.

I didn't know why, but I was treating them

as Mummy had treated me.

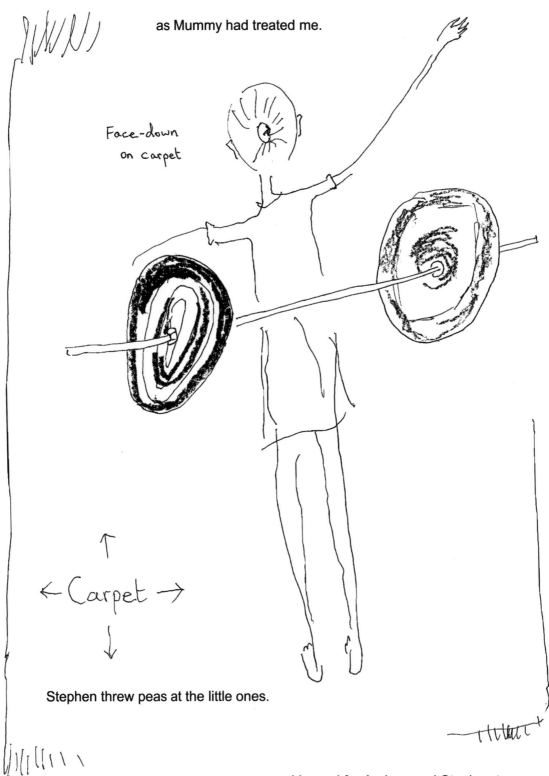

Face-down
on carpet

← Carpet →

Stephen threw peas at the little ones.

I longed for Andrew and Stephen to grow up.

As Keith grew older, Stephen would pull him into a game of Snap.

High speed Snap. No messing about.

'This'll get rid of your anxiety, kid. Come on, you fucking bastard. MOVE!'

Keith watched his step-brother wrench bottle tops off with his teeth.

Stephen's arms had become as thick as my waist.

Stephen had broken a customer's nose at a nightclub.

Keith tried to shut his ears.

Eric ran out.

Stephen's face angered.

'That little brat's going to get it one day.'

But Eric didn't always escape.

He got sprayed with boiling water when Stephen was fiddling with a

carburettor in the garage.

'Hold this, kid, and DON'T drop it. And don't go telling the Idiot. Understand?'

Eric didn't dare move away.

Edward's influence, like a cirrus cloud, hung over the house.

Andrew went off to university to read Theology. Edinburgh.

Wrote letters home.

His father had come back on the scene.

Pooh-poohed everything Andrew was doing.

'Your mother's a nincompoop,' Edward told the trembling youth.

Andrew caught the train at Waverley.

When we met him off the train at Aberdeen he seemed very anxious.

His father wanted him to go to university in Glasgow.

'Engineering!' he told Andrew. 'We don't need Buddha.'

Andrew spoke as if his father was the Dalai Lama.

But he was shivering, and his knees bounced up and down.

He was on the edge of a breakdown.

The GP came to the house and had him admitted to hospital.

That night he took his own life.

CAUSE OF DEATH:
FIRST WORLD WAR

My screams tore my vocal cords.

For twenty days I lost my voice.

I buried my face in his brown waterproof jacket, clutched the belt, the collar.

Buried my face in the empty jacket, for the smell of him, drinking back the

smell of him if I could find any. It couldn't be, that he would never wear that

jacket again. The shape of him, the folds at the elbow, the buttons he'd

fastened.

His books went into the wardrobe. The little boys never used the wardrobe.

School trousers hung on the bedroom door. Denim jackets they chucked on

chairs or threw on the bunk beds.

I lay on the brown and orange mottled carpet. Half the kitchen floor

had carpet, the dining bit. Lay against the storage heater. With a bottle of

wine and swallowed it like the Victoria Falls down my throat. Lay with my eyes

closed.

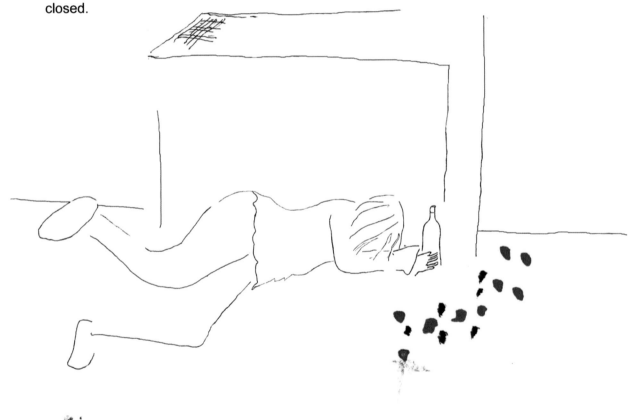

Poured wine down into the pain beyond words. My eyes closed, on

the orange and brown mottled carpet.

After the whisky-laden funeral I felt compelled to sprinkle some of Andrew's ashes at the

Scottish National War Memorial in Edinburgh.

There were reverberations somewhere.

I knew it strongly.

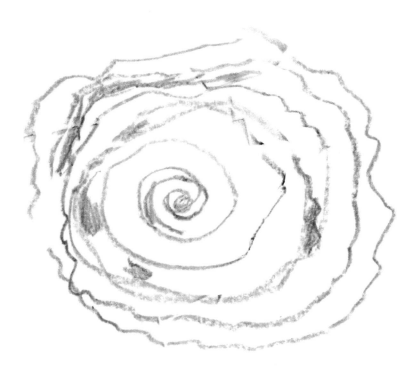

15

Mum moved to Edinburgh.

Transported her grandmother clock and Lladro lady.

Aunty Kate had died.

Aunty Nell was alone.

Grandma had gone years before.

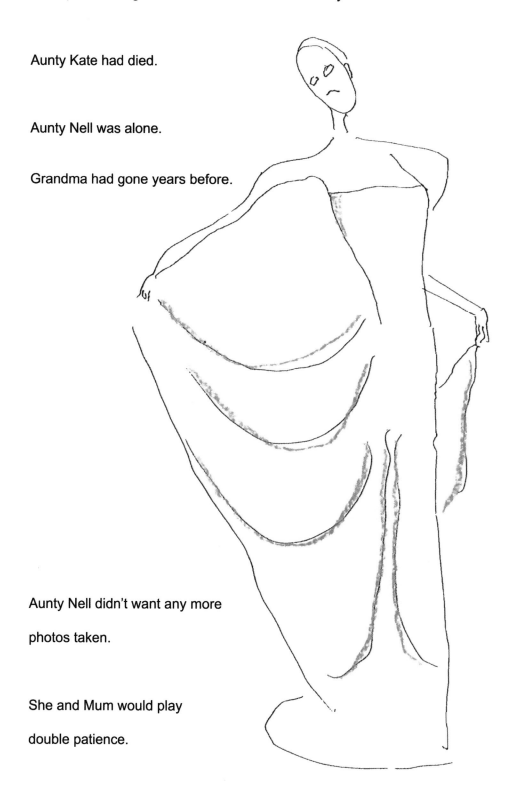

Aunty Nell didn't want any more
photos taken.

She and Mum would play
double patience.

Mum bought herself a flat in Morningside.

Hung her Goose Girl picture on the wall.

Then she noticed people in Morningside had a Harrod's bag and a Jaeger
suit just to go for a pint of milk.

From her kitchen window Mum saw a bowling green with people in white
cardigans.

She took the top off a paracetamol bottle and swallowed a hundred.

At the infirmary they made her feel like a leper.

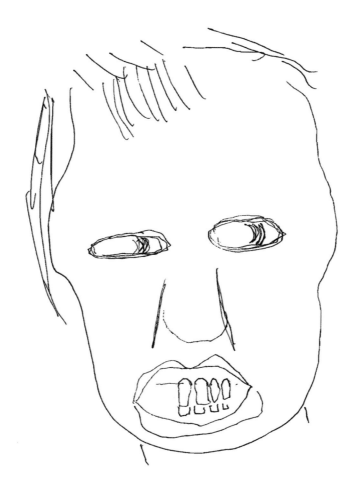

Next came sheltered housing by the Firth of Forth.

Six guests.

But Matron screamed at Mum for hanging out her washing on the wrong day. Even though the line was empty.

Mr Mackintosh, a guest, said Matron's face was like the entrance to the cross-channel ferry.

A ground floor flat in Restalrig came next.

Mum had skipped in Restalrig as a child.

Back to her roots.

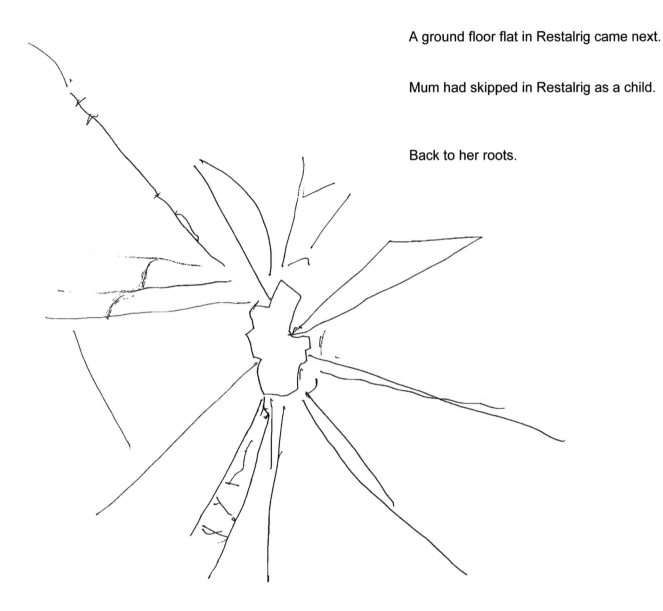

But louts kicked their football against her window.

It was decided Mum would go back to sheltered housing.

Aunty Nell had died.

Absolutely this would be the exact right place.

A flat had come up in Trinity.

People like Virginia Woolf sat in the garden.

Good flower shop.

Mummy was positive this would be her final move.

When I got back from Edinburgh, hammering Rawlplugs and hanging

Mummy's Portmeirion curtains, I went down to our shed.

A misleading article had been in the paper about the Isle of Mull, and

adjoining Erraid.

I had letters in the shed. Our family had historical connections with Erraid.

The shed door handle was held by a rope to a nail.

Painting clothes. Dog guard. Brasso. Rake.

Anti-freeze.

I pulled Mum's box from canes for propping bushes.

A brass box. Stuff from her various moves.

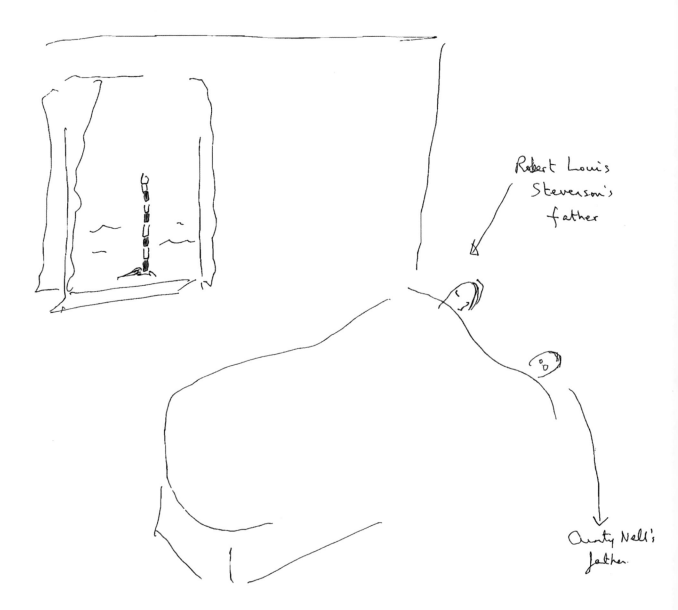

Robert Louis
Stevenson's
father

Aunty Nell's
father.

I could have lived in this shed.

Aunty Nell gave me the letters long ago.

From Aunty Nell's grandad to her father, helping Robert Louis Stevenson's

father build Dubh Artach* lighthouse.

"Dear Son," one said, "we intended To send a loaf Of Bread but we Had to

eat Half."

*pr. 'Doo-Artach'.

But then I saw a book.

As if it had come out of the letter pile.

"John Knox" it said.

John Knox?

Had John Knox been at Mull?

I wasn't Church of Scotland.

What was this for?

Had Mummy thought of reverting to her old religion?

John Knox.

Church leader.

I wondered if Aunty Nell had liked him.

She was a Presbyterian.

As Mummy was before she married.

His house still stands in Edinburgh.

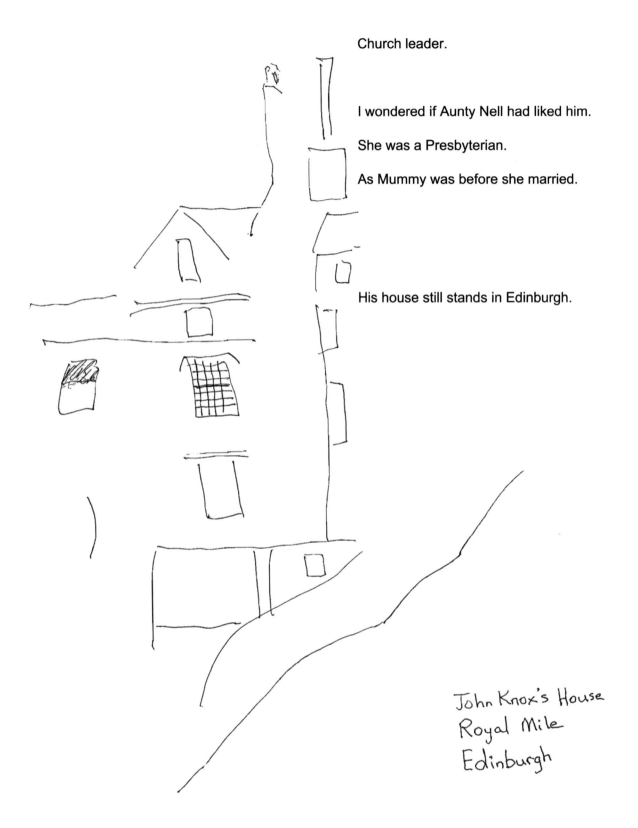

John Knox's House
Royal Mile
Edinburgh

The book opened at Geneva.

I'd popped into Geneva with Sonia.

The Geneva people, I read, were as good as the Apostles.

The Twelve Apostles.

I leaned on the plant-pot shelf.

It said John Knox rowed a boat from Scotland to France.

Edinburgh to France.

On thin soup.

I took the book to the house plus the lighthouse letters I'd almost forgotten

about.

Sprayed Pledge.

Put the book on the radiator.

That night I propped up my V pillow.

And got into the tome.

16

By the third night I knew John Knox had published a book entitled *The Monstrous Regiment of Women.*

I also found John Knox approved of beheadings and being burnt at the stake.

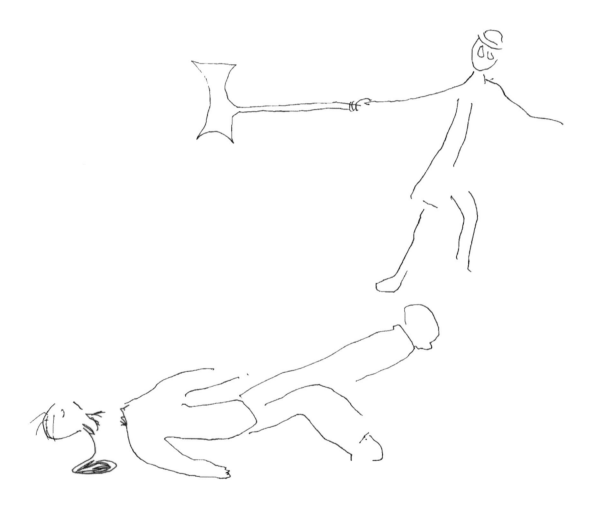

At the stake in Edinburgh?

Edinburgh?

I stared at the long curtains.

A bundle fell on to my duvet.

I jumped as if it was a rat.

It was a list.

It said, "Believed to be dictated by the Lord God to the Blessed John Knox of Scotland."

Blessed John Knox?

Was John Knox a Papist?

I opened it.

"God's Rules For Living"
attributed to the Reverend John Knox

1 Sexual relations are bad.
2 A mother should never coddle her child.
3 Menstruation is disgusting.
4 To deosculate is wicked.
5 To meddle with the pintie is vile.
6 To call someone "Dear" is dreadfully emotional.
7 To hang a garment for restraining the breasts out on the line is unthinkable.
8 Jews should be ostracised.
9 To sit on your father's knee after the age of four is improper.

10 To scream when an educated person abuses one
is a crime.

11 To have the wrong face on for a portrait
is unforgiveable.

12 To look in the mirror is the work of
the devil.

13 To have the wrong colour of hair is
distasteful for others.

14 To have a sense of shame is good.

15 One should set one's face against
mawkish love-making.

16 A bread knife should never be used to
cut turnips or meat.

17 Undergarments are disgusting.

18 Big feet on a woman are abhorrent.

19 Hysteria is for lunatics.

20 The surnames Bottomley or Longbottom
should be altered by deed poll.

21 To be heard defecating will half-kill you.

22 To gaze at a horse having an erection
will blind you.

23 To look at a woman with huge breasts
is abominable.

24 To mention the word "nipple" requires
the mouth to be washed out with vinegar.

I didn't know if nipple and vinegar was the end of the *List*.

But that is all that was there.

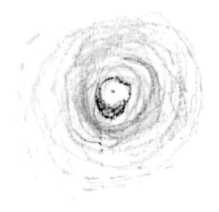

But then suddenly as I re-read the *List*, it started to fade.

Like the Dead Sea Scrolls in Glasgow.

Viewed by torchlight.

"Bottomley" disappeared before my eyes.

I grabbed my dressing gown and raced for brown wrapping paper.

But I never got the wrapping paper.

I landed in hospital.

17

The registrar, Dr Park, asked what I had in the paper package I clasped

like grim death.

Georgie had brought it.

When a nurse touched it I let out a wail as from the Jurassic period and fainted.

They told me the hospital had never heard anything like it.

After I woke from my faint, I nearly passed out again to realise it was the

terrible *list* that meant dusters in my pants, the stealing of my birthright,

the sitting on my father's knee. Everything.

I swooned away a third time.

Mummy came on her rail card from her sheltered housing.

I was muttering about menstruation being disgusting.

Mummy put her face on and went to the tea-room.

I was admitted to a single ward.

With acute existential fragmentation.

The Consultant stood by my bed.

'We have your test results,' he said.

'I think it was the last straw

that broke the camel's back.'

He chuckled.

'I know camels.'

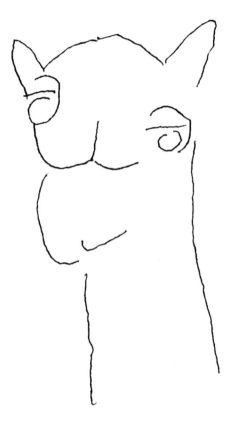

A paper was turned.

'So now. Your List we cannot accept - the wickedness it calls big ears, big feet

- whatever.'

I practised meditation, individual and group therapy and mindfulness.

They said I needed quiet recuperation.

I thought of a friend in the Black Isle. Judith.

And phoned her.

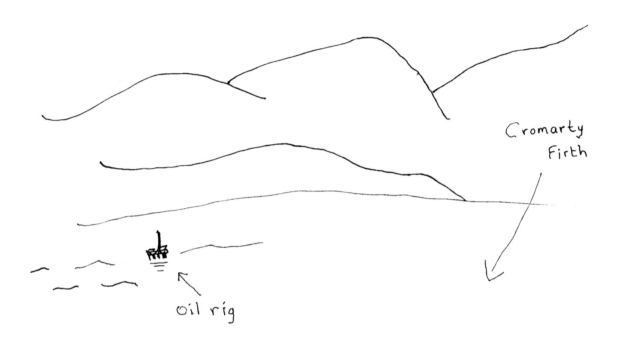

Cromarty Firth

Oil rig

Georgie drove me up to the Black Isle to stay with her.

Judith and I were on the same wavelength.

There was no question about being understood. Bras and big feet. War.

Death.

Her Great Uncle Percy's name was on the Chatham Naval War Memorial for

the Missing near Charles Dickens's home. Thousands of names.

Judith didn't believe in bras.

In my first week Judith woke me at three. To help with a sheep in labour.

I had her late father's dressing gown tied over my pyjamas to venture out in

the cold. I'd never seen a lamb being born.

The waters had broken.

Judith was up to her elbow in fur round its private parts.

I told Judith about my Aunty Nell collecting sheep's poo in a bucket.

One of the jobs I had to do was to hold the animal's umbilical cord.

You couldn't lose an umbilical cord or it might strangle another lamb if there

were two.

After the lamb I felt greatly strengthened.

I felt it was a symbol of inspiration.

In the mornings I stood on the verandah and fastened the belt of truth and

shield of faith round me.

Goldberg Variations floated from the sitting room.

I stayed with my friend four weeks.

Over mugs of hot chocolate we discussed my Turkish grudge. Mum taking

a hundred paracetamol.

Ancestors.

The *List*.

'You should make a bonfire,' said Judith. 'When you get home burn the whole

evil of the List. Burn it!'

I had nothing to say.

'But your mother wasn't all bad,' said Judith.

'She put hot water bottles in our beds,' I said.

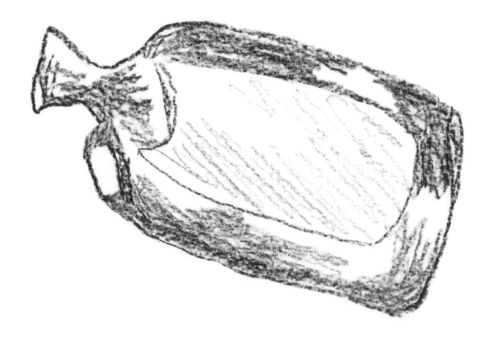

'When you've finished', went on Judith, you could say, 'Come, all beauty of

creation. Into me!'

I got home with my new head. During the holiday we'd talked about Keith.

The sobs and struggle when I tried to make him join the Cubs.

'Be normal!' I'd shrieked.

And flung him a grubby duster from cleaning the windscreen.

For his tears.

But that was all in the past.

Next day I did my bonfire in the garden.

I took a pile of names.

All sickness in the family going back to

great great great great grandparents. The inherited chromosomes

they'd suspected in blood tests. I threw in Turkey who killed

Mummy's warm and loving father, and the Sutherland cult.

I flung in John Knox and his rowing boat, tossed the

writer of the *List* and then tipped sticks and

potato peelings, an empty All Bran box and

a cardboard toilet roll tube

over the lot.

18

From now on things would be different.

We had raked the coals of my past.

Keith had left school with one O-Level.

Art.

Utterly vague about his future.

But that was alright.

My brother knew the manager of Fine Fare.

Keith got a job stacking shelves.

But within six months the Fine Fare job had gone up in smoke.

Keith was observed lifting a tin as if moving a hamster or a baby bird.

Moved his arm slowly, straightened his trousers, coughed and covered his mouth with the back of his hand, concentrated on doing the best job at shelf-stacking that anybody had ever done.

Was my bonfire not working?

He signed on at the dole.

He lay in bed all day.

That was ok.

I could cope.

He drew a jester on his bedroom wall.

spatula →

He went in and out of hospital.

Sectioned.

Electroconvulsive therapy.

**24
HOURS**

I wondered what was going on.

I tried to live one day at a time.

But I eventually cracked.

I asked our minister about exorcism.

The Reverend Hallow said he would

come to our son's bedroom.

Holy Communion, Mr Hallow said, was more powerful

than exorcism.

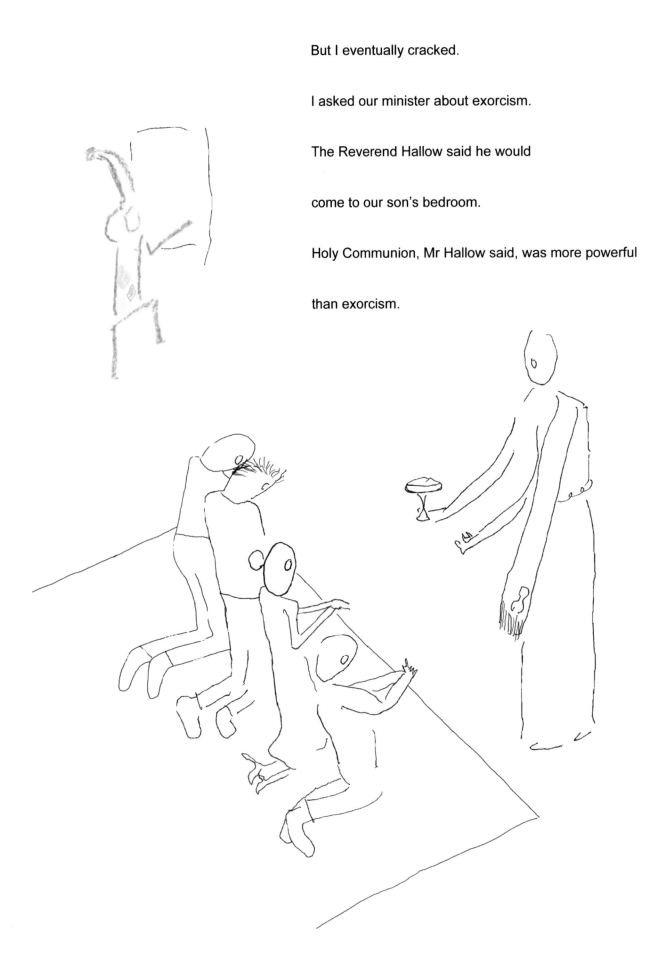

So that was that.

A flight of angels winged through the house.

We gave Keith a workroom. Full of hope.

He said he wanted to fix the inside of an old speaker to a new one.

But the first night there was a crash of splintering wood.

Like Forestry Commission trees being felled at Drumnadrochit.

We took a packet of Werther's and a hi-fi magazine to the hospital.

But our son was screaming in his side-ward and trying to climb up the wall.

There was blue paint all over the carpet he said.

The nurse said Keith was difficult.

But there WAS wet paint all over the carpet.

Wet paint.

It was completely inexplicable.

Totally surreal.

I wanted to phone Judith.

Would it be on the car's accelerator?

Was this what was called Folie à Deux? Some crazy Folie à Trois?

Georgie and I came back at night with scrubbing brushes and detergent.

Never spoke a word.

We got home after eleven.

19

Then out of the blue a Housing Association gave Keith a flat!

On a lovely estate.

B&Q and Sainsbury's far below.

From the hall you could see the sea.

We drove to Kosy Carpets.

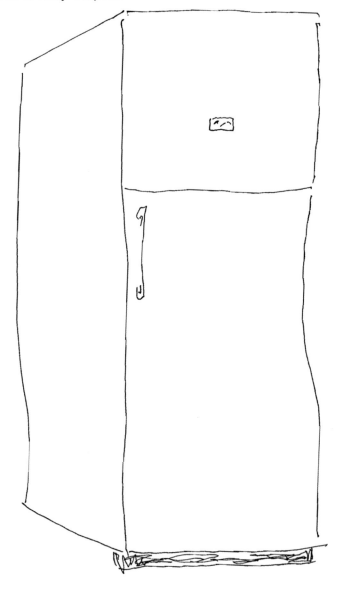

If he did his own windows and had his own fridge Keith might feel more

purpose.

But we found he was smoking cannabis.

And had been for years.

Though wasn't half of London on cocaine?

His needs were met by two middle-aged dealers who never moved from the

front of their parents' fire and TV.

But I was very nervous.

And more so when we learnt Keith's present supplies came from a man he'd met

in hospital.

Pins in his nose.

Tattoos.

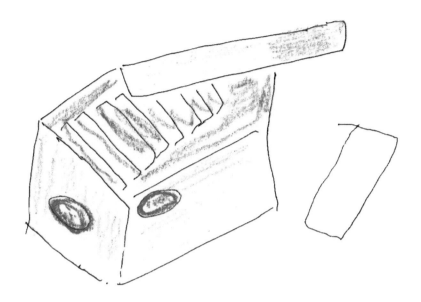

The hospital person's name was Merlin.

It was visiting hour.

'Merlin?'

I had leaned forward.

'I get forty condoms a month.'

'Really,' I said.

My mother came up.

I went to the corner shop.

My next door neighbour was buying cigarettes.

My neighbour said the cottage three doors up was for sale.

I came back from the corner shop.

I told my Mum the house three doors up was for sale.

We got the key.

She bought it.

I couldn't believe it!

On my doorstep!

In went the Lladro lady and the Parker Knoll.

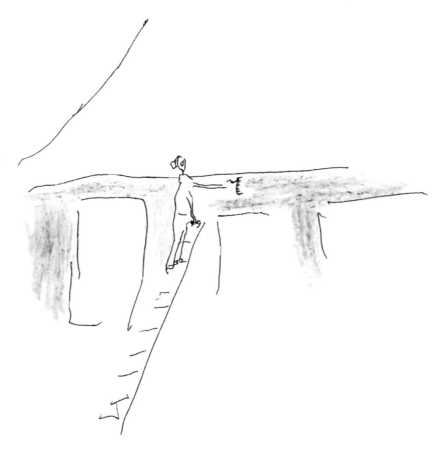

I painted her house pink.

But we still weren't out of the woods.

The Housing Association flat started going to the dogs.

Keith took four hours for a shower. A slave to his OCD.

The hot tank was like a galloping horse in the Grand National.

A cupboard fell off the kitchen wall.

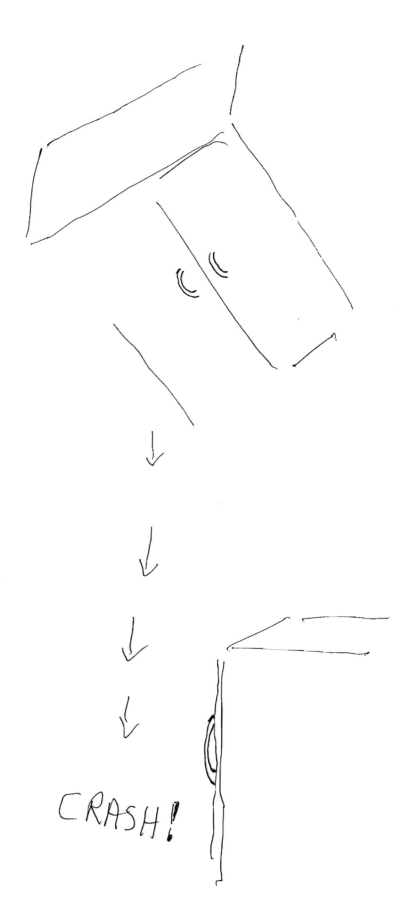

CRASH!

But apart from these nightmares I was thankful Mummy was happy.

She had a wartime photo of Daddy beside her alcove bed.

"With all my love now and forever. John. xxxxxxxxxx"

Mummy and I played Scrabble every night.

It was Mummy's favourite game.

It wasn't my favourite game.

But I played it with good grace.

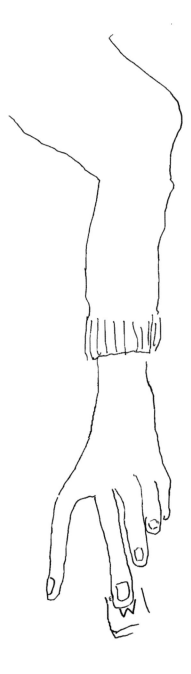

Then one night I saw her index finger as she

placed a tile.

The filed oval.

No paint.

Clean.

Innocent.

Something happened to my inside.

'Your turn,' she said softly.

And I knew like the morning dawn that my efforts had worked.

I didn't quite know how.

I was different.

Had she sensed it?

But she was also different.

I placed my letter on a triple square and looked up.

Then widened my eyes.

My mother wore a crown on her head!

She looked up too.

The crown faded.

I think it was similar to the Bishop and the dove.

20

But then the next onslaught arrived.

Merlin from the hospital took a bottle of Southern Comfort to Keith's new flat.

And brought up his hospital dinner on Keith's sitting room carpet.

I couldn't believe it.

The hospital heard of the disaster.

A girl drew up in a red car.

To see Keith.

Yes, he was here.

We'd never met anyone so full of beans.

A Community Support Social Person.

Keith hid in the bathroom.

But the following week Keith and the Social Support girl, Karen, had climbed

Bennachie together.

Saw rabbits.

The girl had made sandwiches.

Sandwiches.

Was this really happening?

Keith said a rainbow appeared.

By the end of the week he had fallen in love.

He asked if I thought he should write and tell the girl she was "wondrous".

I felt quite overwhelmed that Keith would trust my reply.

My son's soul stood naked. His eyes shone like the outermost star.

'She IS, Mum.'

'I believe you.'

'Will I write and tell her?'

I couldn't get it out of my head that this girl might be the long-awaited

answer.

There might be a marriage.

Grandchildren.

A little dog running around.

After the letter Keith never saw the object of his desire again.

Vanished off the map.

He was devastated.

The girl had been transferred to Dundee.

Next day Keith was dead.

There was a partial eclipse of the sun at his funeral.

His face was a sunflower.

But childhood damage had struck at the roots.

The roots couldn't support it.

CAUSE OF DEATH:

FIRST WORLD WAR

21

Ten days later Mummy had a heart attack in the night.

But she wouldn't phone till 8.

It wasn't correct to disturb people.

Red zig-zags ran over her cardiology screen.

For two hours.

Then stopped.

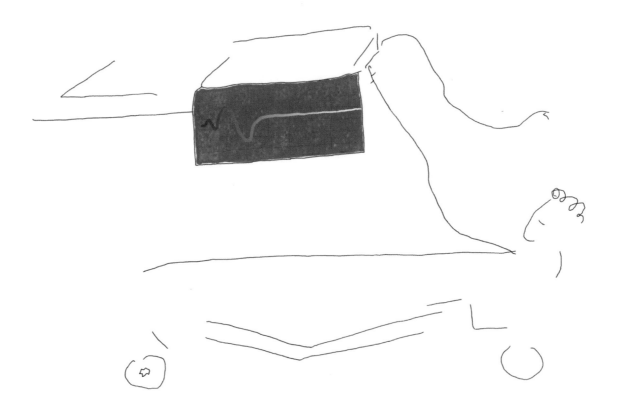

Her hands were together.

I closed her eyes.

Everything right.

Blow-dry the previous day.

Marky's nightie.

The nurses ripped the polythene and the receipt.

I barely breathed.

Epilogue

Later that year I arranged to send a goat to Turkey.

Anglo-Nubian.

They could make yogurt from the milk - start a business.

(General Secretary Muslim Aid

PLEASE FORWARD THIS TO TURKISH GOVERNMENT)

218 Desswood Place
Aberdeen
AB10 4TT
UK

Right Hon. General Secretary
Turkish Government
Istanbul

Dear Sir,

Please accept a gift of a goat I am sending to your country as a token of
recompence. Perhaps you could give it to some poor people in the Gallipoli
Peninsula where my Grandad died.

Your army killed my Grandad in the 1st World War.

But grudges get us nowhere. I ask to be forgiven, Sir, that I have hated
your country all my life.

The goat will arrive by Animal Airlines at Ataturk Airport.
Date and time of arrival under separate cover.

I hope Turkey gets into the EU.

Yours sincerely
(Mrs) Betty Turnbull.

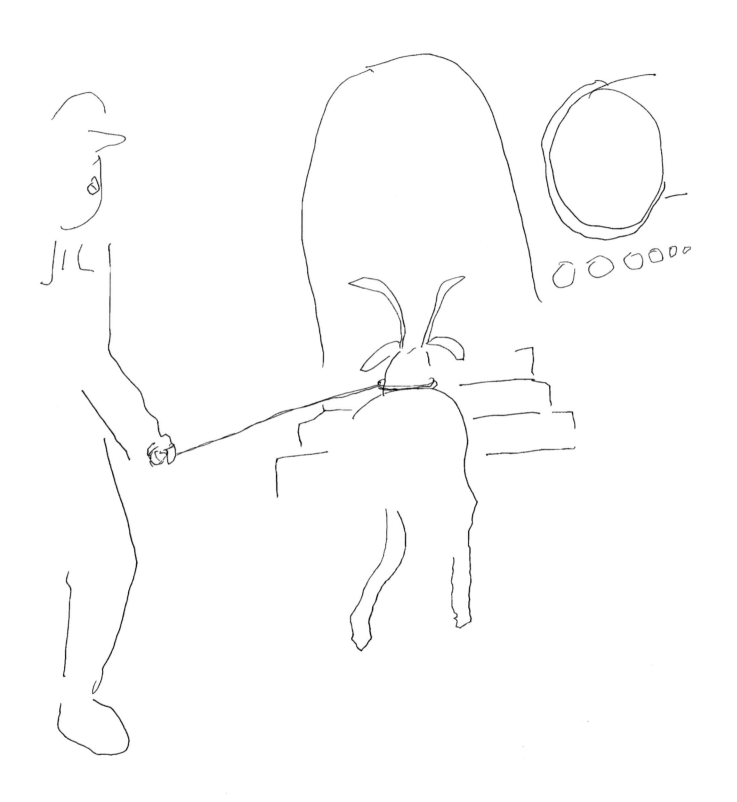

Digital conversion and formatting

by Ben Duff